Every day Elmo learns how to do something new.

To Luke,
Love from Mama

Library of Congress Cataloging-in-Publication Data
Alexander, Liza.
Surprise, Mommy! / by Liza Alexander ; illustrated by David Prebenna.
p. cm. — (Elmo's World) "Featuring Jim Henson's Sesame Street Muppets."
SUMMARY: Daddy helps Elmo make a surprise gift for Mommy—a batch of jiggly "gelmo."
ISBN 0-679-89423-3 (trade) — ISBN 0-679-99423-8 (lib. bdg.)
[1. Gifts—Fiction. 2. Parent and child—Fiction. 3. Puppets—Fiction.]
I. Prebenna, David, ill. II. Title. III. Series. PZ7.A37735Su 1999 dc21 [E] 98-49494

www.randomhouse.com/kids
www.sesamestreet.com
CTW BOOKS is a trademark of CTW Publishing Company LLC.

Printed in Mexico 10 9 8 7 6 5 4 3 2 1

Surprise, Mommy!

by Liza Alexander

illustrated by
David Prebenna

Featuring Jim Henson's Sesame Street Muppets

CTW Books

Every morning, Mommy gives Elmo a wake-up hug.

Elmo's favorite breakfast is Monster Flakes. Mommy pours the milk. Then she lets Elmo sprinkle the sugar.

Then it's time to go. Elmo knows how to put on his jacket all by himself, but sometimes Mommy helps.

Every night Elmo has a bath. On special nights
Mommy lets him have two caps of bubbles.

Mommy dries Elmo's fur and cuddles him in a towel.
Elmo thinks, "Mommy is nice to Elmo all through the
day. Elmo will give Mommy a surprise present. Then
Mommy will know that Elmo love-love-loves her. But
what would Mommy like?"

All the next day Elmo think-think-thinks. Maybe Mommy would like a rocket pop? Maybe Mommy would like a dump truck that really dumps? Maybe she'd like a robot? Or a pair of sneakers that light up?

That night, Elmo tells Daddy his ideas for a present. Elmo wonders, "Which one is the nicest for Mommy?"

Daddy answers, "All of those things are nice. But do you know what Mommy likes best? Presents that Elmo makes all by himself."

During sleepytime, even while he's dreaming, Elmo think-think-thinks.

The next morning, Mommy has work to do. She sets up her project in the dining room.

Daddy and Elmo clean up the kitchen. Elmo sees something. He points to a box in the cupboard. "That's what Elmo will make for Mommy!"

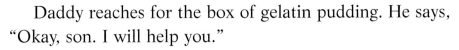

Daddy reaches for the box of gelatin pudding. He says, "Okay, son. I will help you."

"Mommy will love her gelmo!" says Elmo. "It will be a special surprise."

When Elmo tears open the packet, the powder poofs
into the air. "Uh-oh!"

Elmo's red fur has turned purple with powder. "Daddy,
what will we do?" he asks.

"Don't worry," says Daddy. He helps Elmo brush off his fur. "There's enough left for Mommy's gelmo."

Elmo carefully measures water and ice cubes.

Then Daddy helps Elmo pour the cold mix into the hot purple gelmo water.

Elmo picks out a beautiful bowl and Daddy pours in the gelmo. Daddy lets Elmo put the bowl in the fridge all by himself.

Elmo has another idea. "The surprise present needs a card. And on the card will be a poem. Elmo will write it!" Daddy helps with the poem. Elmo signs it with his name.

Elmo peeks in the fridge. The gelmo still isn't ready!
Daddy has to go do an errand. Elmo stays.

He waits and waits and waits.

"Maybe Elmo should test it and see if the gelmo's okay?"
Elmo pokes his finger in and takes a taste. He makes a hole.
Then he tests again. He makes another hole. And another.

"Now Elmo should smooth it out." Elmo gets a spoon.
He smoothes the gelmo. Then he takes another taste. Then
he smoothes it out again. Soon there isn't much gelmo left.

Now Elmo is worried. The gelmo for Mommy doesn't look right. Only a little bit is left, and that little bit is all lumpy.

Elmo has an idea. He decides to wrap the bowl up with pretty paper and a bow. Maybe the gelmo won't look so bad now. Daddy comes home from his errand.

"Surprise, Mommy!" says Elmo.

Mommy reads her card. She smiles. She tastes her gelmo.
"Do you like your present?" asks Elmo.
"Yes, Elmo," answers Mommy. "It's very sweet. But do you know what's even sweeter?"
"No, Mommy, what?"

"My little Elmo!" says Mommy.

Every day Elmo learns how to do something new.
Today, he learned how to give a present.